This SPECIAL STORIES BOOK Belongs To:

_____

P/6/2191599.

Published in 2009 by
Special Stories Publishing

Member of CLÉ - The Irish Book Publishers Association

Design by Graham Thew Design www.grahamthew.com

ISBN 978 0 9561751 1 3

A catalogue record for this book is available from the British Library

Printed By C&C Offset Printing Co. Ltd., China

Special Stories Publishing
www.specialstories.ie

FREDDIE'S SUPER SUMMER

By Kate Gaynor

Illustrated by Aileen Murphy

Hi! My name is Freddie and this is my friend Jerry.

Me and Jerry became friends last summer at a summer camp near my school.

Summer camp is a bit like school but instead of teachers there are camp leaders who are there to make sure you have fun!

There are lots of different activities every day like fancy dress, making funny hats or just playing games with all your new friends.

I had planned to go to camp that summer with my best friend Mark, but Mark got sick with measles and instead I had to go to summer camp alone. On my first day, Mum came with me to meet the camp leaders. It felt like my first day of school all over again.

"Have a great time Freddie," Mum called from the car window as she drove away. "How can I have a great time when I don't even have a friend here?" I thought sadly.

On the first day of summer camp the team leaders
divided us into different teams. Everyone else in my team
seemed to know each other and I felt kind of left out and
a little bit lonely. The only boy I recognised on
my team was Jerry.

Jerry joined our school last year and on his first day
Teacher told us to take extra care that Jerry didn't feel
left out. But my friends and I were always too busy with
our own games to ask Jerry to join in.

The second day at summer camp was a dressing up day. Jerry sometimes talked too loudly because he found it hard to hear. "Pirate!" he shouted when the box of funny clothes arrived. Jerry loved dressing up and having fun. He always wanted everyone else to join in too. I think that's the reason he had so many friends at summer camp.

"Everyone has to wait their turn Jerry," said Tim our team leader. "What about you Freddie, what would you like to be?" Even though I really liked dressing up, I told Tim I didn't want to play. I just wasn't sure if I wanted to join in

While I was sitting on my own staring out of the window, I heard a voice behind me. I knew it was Jerry because his voice sounds a little different than the other boys and girls. Sometimes he finds it hard to say some of his words. "For you," he said with a big smile as he handed me a cowboy costume.

Jerry put a pirate's patch over his eye. "Look, a pirate" he
laughed. Jerry always seemed to be happy and smiling
and I couldn't help smiling too.

The next day was 'funny hat' day. Everyone brought in a hat to decorate so it would look as silly as it could be! "Where's your hat, Freddie?" asked Tim the team leader, "I didn't bring one," I said.

"Have my hat!" said Jerry loudly as he pulled the hat down over his eyes and did a little dance. "That's very kind of you to share your hat with Freddie," said Tim. "Yes, thanks Jerry," I said with a smile.

Later that day when my Dad collected me from camp, Jerry was outside with his Mum and some of his friends. Jerry was never too shy to make new friends. "Bye Freddie!" he shouted loudly. "Have you made a new friend?" asked Dad. "No," I said grumpily, "that's Jerry, he's just in my team."

"It's so hard to make friends at summer camp," I told Dad
on the way home. "Jerry is great at making friends".
"Maybe that's because Jerry is always so kind to
everyone," said Dad. When I looked back from the
window of the car Jerry was still smiling and
waving at me from the gate.

The next day at camp, all the teams came together on the grass. "Today we are going to have a big sports day for all the teams at summer camp," said Tim the team leader.

"We need teams of two people to run in the three legged race," said Tim. "Me, me, me!" shouted Jerry. "That's great Jerry," said Tim. "Who wants to run the race with Jerry?" "I do" I said. "Well done Freddie," said Tim, "it's great to see you joining in".

From that day on summer camp was just great! Jerry helped me to see how important it is that everyone in the group always joins in. That way no-one ever feels left out.

Later that day Jerry and I won the three legged race.
And everyone in our team clapped and cheered.
Jerry cheered the loudest of all! I just can't wait for
summer camp next year. Why don't you
come along too?

YOUR SPECIAL STORY PAGE

NOTES FOR GROWN UP'S:

DOWN SYNDROME: A syndrome is a name used for a collection of several features that usually occur together. The name Down syndrome comes from Dr. John Langdon Down, an English doctor who first described the characteristic features of this syndrome. Almost 100 years later, Professor Lejeune (Paris 1959) discovered why children with Down syndrome share characteristics in appearance and have degrees of developmental delays and recognisable characteristics. The reason is based in the chromosome make-up. The three forms of Down syndrome are called simple trisomy, translocation and mosaicism. As yet it is not known what causes Down syndrome.

HOW TO USE THIS BOOK:

WHEN A CHILD WITH Down syndrome joins a mainstream school many children can find it difficult to understand a student that is somewhat 'different' to them. While the story encourages other children to be mindful and patient of the differences that exist between them, the story's main focus is to portray the many positive personality traits of a child with Down syndrome and shows how their inspiring and uplifting their contribution to a group can be.

DOWN SYNDROME IRELAND:

Down Syndrome Ireland promotes inclusion, equality and choices for people with Down syndrome and their families. People experience many great things and also face many challenges throughout their lives. People with Down syndrome are no different, but may need a little extra help and support along the way. Down Syndrome Ireland's goal is to help people with Down syndrome make their own futures as bright and independent as possible by providing them with education, support and friendship every step of the way.

For further information please contact

Down Syndrome Ireland,
Citylink Business Park,
Old Naas Road,
Dublin 12
Tel: (01) 426 6500
Email: info@downsyndrome.ie

Acknowledgements:

Many thanks to the Special Stories Publishing advisory Board, Michael Gill, Sandra O'Malley, Aine Lynch, David Shaw, Fintan Maher, Paul Toner and to Social Entrepreneurs Ireland, Sean, Lynda, Claire and Annalisa for all of their encouragement, advice and unwavering support. Many thanks also to Kieran O'Donoghue, Michael & George Gaynor and our extended family and friends, Liam Gaynor, Liz O'Donoghue, Trevor Patterson and Aileen Murphy, Graham Thew, James Fitzsimons and Tony Bond.

Special Stories Publishing is supported by Social Entrepreneurs Ireland
www.socialentrepreneurs.ie

Special thanks to John Lindsay, Margaret O'Carroll and Down Syndrome Ireland without whose involvement this book would have not been possible.

Special thanks also to Dr. Imelda Coyne, Trinity College Dublin whose time and effort with this project was so greatly appreciated.

About the Author:

Kate Gaynor is the author of 11 published children's books. Her titles address the issues of children with special education needs or health and social problems. She works closely with healthcare professionals, psychologists, teachers and families on a daily basis to ensure the quality of her work. Kate is an English and Sociology graduate of University College Dublin and lives and works in Dublin, Ireland

About the Illustrator:

Aileen Murphy is an Artist who lives in Dublin. She grew up in the country side of Wicklow and then studied in the The National College of Art and Design. Now she works in her studio in Dublin City drawing and making various 3D Art. Aileen's artwork usually relates to Fairy tales, girlhood motifs and wacky dreams.

Other Books from SPECIAL STORIES PUBLISHING

The SPECIAL STORIES SERIES 2:

THE SPECIAL STORIES SERIES 2 – These books are designed to introduce all children to the positive aspects of inclusive education with each book featuring a character with a certain special education need. The stories help children to learn the importance of accepting friends and classmates who are 'different' to them.

A BIRTHDAY FOR BEN

Children with hearing difficulties. It's Ben's 7th birthday, but he really doesn't want a birthday party! When his friends surprise him, he then learns just how easy it is for everyone to join in the fun.

TOM'S SPECIAL TALENT

Dyslexia/Learning difficulties. Tom isn't sure if he really has any talents at all when he sees how good his friends are at reading and writing. But a school competition helps him to find his own very 'special talent'.

FREDDIE'S SUPER SUMMER

Down Syndrome. It's Freddie's very first time at summer camp and he's certain he won't enjoy it or make friends. But it isn't long before a boy called Jerry helps him to see otherwise!

A FRIEND LIKE SIMON:

Autism/ASD. When a new boy joins Matthew's school, he's just not sure if he wants to have a friend like Simon. But a school trip to the funfair soon helps to change his mind!

(Books are sold separately and/or as part of a box set)

The SPECIAL STORIES SERIES 1:

A FAMILY FOR SAMMY
Foster Care

FIRST PLACE
Cleft Palate & Speech difficulties

THE LOST PUPPY
Limited mobility/ wheelchair users

THE FAMOUS HAT
Childhood Cancer

JOE'S SPECIAL STORY
Inter-country Adoption

THE WINNER
Asthma

THE BRAVEST GIRL IN SCHOOL
Diabetes

(Books are sold separately and/or as part of a box set)

www.specialstories.ie

www.specialstories.ie